WHO WANTS A PANCAKE?

None of the cubs at Bear Country School do. That's because the "pancake" is the favorite wrestling move of Milton Chubb, the huge new cub.

Milton and Bertha Broom have been drawn together by their farm backgrounds and by their matching sizes. But there's rough going ahead for the king-size love-birds. Will Too-Tall's teasing break them up? Or will they be torn apart by their own competition for the heavyweight spot on the school's new wrestling team?

BIG CHAPTER BOOKS

The Berenstain Bears and the LOVE MATCH

by the Berenstains

A BIG CHAPTER BOOK™

Random House New York

Copyright © 1998 by Berenstain Enterprises, Inc.

All rights reserved under International and Pan-American Copyright Conventions. Published in the United States by Random House, Inc., New York, and simultaneously in Canada by Random House of Canada Limited, Toronto.

http://www.randomhouse.com/
http://www.berenstainbears.com/

Library of Congress Cataloging-in-Publication Data
Berenstain, Stan, 1923–
The Berenstain Bears and the love match / by the Berenstains.
    p. cm. — (A big chapter book)
Summary: Big Brother helps Milton Chubb, a huge new cub, deal with the school bully and make friends with Bertha Broom, but then Milton and Bertha must meet in a match for a spot on the school's wrestling team.
ISBN 0-679-88942-6 (trade) — ISBN 0-679-98942-0 (lib. bdg.)
[1. Bears—Fiction. 2. Schools—Fiction. 3. Bullies—Fiction. 4. Wrestling—Fiction.] I. Berenstain, Jan, 1923–   . II. Title. III. Series: Berenstain, Stan, 1923–   Big chapter book.
PZ7.B4483Bejlf 1998
[Fic]—dc21
97-38410

Printed in the United States of America 10 9 8 7 6 5 4 3 2 1

BIG CHAPTER BOOKS is a trademark of Berenstain Enterprises, Inc.

Contents

Chapter 1
Massive Milton

As towns go, Beartown was a rather small one. That made Bear Country School, as schools go, a pretty small school. Most of the cubs there knew each other, and most of the new cubs each year were the incoming kindergartners who were the brothers and sisters of cubs in the higher grades.

But every once in a while, a different kind of new cub appeared at school: a cub whose family had just moved to Beartown.

To such a cub, every other cub in the school was a total stranger. That made it kind of hard to adjust to school life. And it was especially hard for a new cub who looked unusual in some way. No cub knew that better than Harry "Wheels" McGill. Harry's legs had been injured in an auto accident when he was a little cub, and he had to use a wheelchair to get around. That made other cubs uncomfortable around him at first. All except for Too-Tall and his gang. They weren't uncomfortable around him— they just teased him without mercy.

Ever since his difficult experience, Harry had taken a special interest in helping other new cubs adjust. But he suspected that his wheelchair made new cubs uncomfortable, so he usually teamed up with Brother Bear and his friends, the cubs who had helped him in his own ordeal. That's why, at this very moment, Harry was steering his wheelchair across the crowded school playground to where Brother and friends were talking.

"Hi, Wheels," said Brother. "What's up?"

"Something's comin' down, that's what's up," said Harry.

"I object," sniffed Ferdy Factual, peering through his thick lenses at Harry. "A thing cannot be both up and down at the same time. It's a contradiction in terms. Unless, of course, you're speaking about quantum physics—"

"I'll give you a contradiction right in the

nose, Ferd," said Harry good-naturedly. "No time for wordplay. We've got to act fast." He pointed across the playground to a cluster of girl cubs gathered closely around a boy cub who stood head and shoulders above them.

"Wow," said Brother. "Kinda tall, isn't he?"

"That's not all he is," said Harry. "He's also wide. *Very* wide. His name's Milton."

"*Milton?*" said Barry Bruin. "He's gonna get teased about that name."

"Not to mention his weight," said Harry. "And, to top it all off, he's also very shy. Look, Too-Tall and the gang are coming up the road now. I want you guys to make friends with Milton before they get here and start messin' with him. But *no* remarks about his weight. *Or* his clothes. Got that?"

The cubs nodded. "Don't worry," said

Brother. "We'll all just say, 'Hi, Milton. It's very nice to meet you.'"

"Good," said Harry. "A little stiff, but good. Come on."

As they approached the cluster, they could hear the girls' voices, high and shrill.

Queenie McBear: "Oh, Milton, you're such a *big* bear on campus!" Babs Bruno: "I'm sure you're just as *big*-hearted as you are *big*, Milton!" Bermuda McBear: "May I put my arms around you, Milton? Never mind, I don't think they'll *go* all the way around!" Each tease was greeted by a gale of squeals and giggles and by a deeper reddening of Milton's broad face.

"What are you girls up to?" scolded Harry.

Queenie looked over her shoulder at Harry in mock surprise. "We're just havin' a little ol' blushing contest," she said. "With Milton as the only contestant!" More squealing and giggling.

"Well, break it up," said Harry. "It's time for Milton to meet some of the guys."

The cluster of girls parted, revealing Milton in all his glory. Brother could see why

Harry was concerned for the poor guy. He was wearing a pair of overalls. And he wasn't just tall and wide. He was *enormous*.

Brother stepped forward to be introduced first.

"Milton," said Harry, "I want you to meet a good friend of mine, Brother Bear." Milton thrust his meaty hand at Brother as Harry continued, "Brother, this is Milton Chubb."

Brother had his opening line well memorized by now, but hearing Milton's last name threw him off balance. He grasped the new cub's hand and said, "Hi, Milton. It's very fat to meet you."

Bonnie Brown gasped. Harry looked at Brother in horror. Milton's ongoing blush turned a deeper shade of red.

"And this," said Harry quickly, pulling Ferdy forward, "is Ferdy Factual. He's our resident genius and nephew of the great scientist Actual Factual."

Again Milton put out his huge hand. "Gee," he said softly. "It's an honor, Ferdy."

Ferdy, delighted at the respect he was being shown, smiled and shook Milton's

OUCH!

hand. But he too could not get Milton's last name out of his mind. "Thank you very large," he said, then added, "Ouch!" as Cousin Fred elbowed him in the ribs.

"Way to go, Brother and Ferdy!" boomed a familiar voice behind them. Too-Tall and his gang had arrived. "You sure got off a couple of zingers there!"

Brother said quickly, "But we didn't mean—"

"*Of course*, you didn't," sneered Too-Tall. "You straight arrows would *never* stoop to making fun of a new cub, would you?" He looked Milton up and down. The cub was as tall as he was and much heavier. "Well, look what the cat dragged in—or maybe I should say *lion*." The gang snickered. Too-Tall frowned and tapped his chin with a forefinger. "Nah. Let's forget about cats altogether. Look what the *elephant* dragged in!"

The rest of the gang doubled over in fits of laughter.

"Come on, big guy," pleaded Harry, who was Too-Tall's best chess buddy. "Be nice."

"Be *what?*" said Too-Tall. "You gotta be kiddin'! I couldn't be nice if I tried. It ain't in my nature." He turned back to the new cub. "What's your name, big fella?"

Milton cleared his throat. "Milton Chubb," he said softly.

Skuzz, Smirk, and Vinnie rolled around on the blacktop, roaring with laughter. Too-Tall just grinned broadly. "What was that?" he said, cupping his hand behind his ear. "I didn't quite get that—Milton Blubber, was it?"

The new cub was blushing so hard now you could almost see steam rising from his head. "Chubb," he muttered, looking at the ground.

"Oh, *Chubb!*" said Too-Tall. "Chubb's the name, *fat's* his game! But he needs a nickname, too."

"I know, boss!" cried Skuzz. "Let's make him a gang member! I'll even let him be your right-hand bear. The two of you would be great together. Too-Tall and...Too-*Fat!*"

When the crowd's laughter had died down, Too-Tall waved a hand. "Nah. I got a better nickname." He stepped forward and brought his right hand down on the new cub's shoulder in a slow karate-chop motion. "I dub thee...Massive Milton!"

I DUB THEE · · · MASSIVE MILTON !

Harry, Brother, and Bonnie gritted their teeth as they watched Milton fix his gaze on the blacktop before him. He seemed to be trying to burn a hole in it with his eyes so he could climb in and hide.

"Wait a minute," said Too-Tall, sniffing the air. "What's that I smell?"

Vinnie hurried to Too-Tall's side. He had the gang's sharpest nose. "Smells like a combination of hay and chicken feed, boss," he announced.

Too-Tall looked up at Milton. "You wouldn't happen to live on a farm, would you?" he asked.

"My dad and mom are the new hands at Farmer Ben's," said Milton. "I help them out."

"You know, you really ought to take a shower before you come to school," said Too-Tall in a helpful tone of voice.

Milton's eyebrows raised. "I did," he said.

"Well, tomorrow take *two*," said Too-Tall. "Like I always say, Milt. The first test you have to pass at Bear Country School is the *sniff* test. Let's go, gang."

As they strolled away, Too-Tall looked back and called, "Hang with us after school, Miltie! We'll show you the town!"

"I don't know about that, boss!" shouted Skuzz for all to hear. "How they gonna keep him down on the farm after he's seen Beartown?"

When they'd gone, Harry eased his wheelchair up to Milton. "If you haven't already guessed," he said, "that was our resident gang leader and bully. Sorry you had to meet him so soon."

Just then the morning bell rang, signaling the start of school.

"If you're in Teacher Bob's class," said Brother, "we'll walk with you."

Milton just looked around the group of cubs, then stared off at Too-Tall and the gang. "Smart-aleck city cubs," he muttered. He turned and trudged off alone to the schoolhouse entrance.

Brother caught Harry's eye, and they both sighed and shook their heads. It wasn't going to be easy helping Milton Chubb adjust to Bear Country School.

Chapter 2
Shy Guy

Brother, Harry, and their friends thought Milton's remark about "city cubs" a bit odd until they heard about the new cub's background in Teacher Bob's class. Whenever a new cub joined the class, Teacher Bob asked him to stand up and say a little about himself. It turned out that the Chubbs came from a farming area whose biggest town consisted of a few homes, a gas station, a mom-and-pop grocery store, and a feed store. The nearest Greybear Bus station was twenty miles away. So, to Milton, Beartown must have seemed like a big city.

Unfortunately, Milton didn't make a good impression on the class when he rose to speak. His shyness got in the way. Teacher Bob had to pull every little bit of information out of him by asking questions. Soon Milton began to blush again. It didn't help that most of the class was whispering and snickering. Especially the girls. The only girl who wasn't, besides Bonnie Brown, was Bertha Broom. Bertha was almost as big as Milton and had lived on a farm for years before coming to Beartown. She looked up at Milton with interest and admiration as Teacher Bob asked questions. Seeing her rapt attention might have boosted the confidence of a cub less shy with girls than Milton. But as soon as she caught Milton's eye, he blushed more deeply and his knees started to shake.

"Tim-ber-r-r!" shouted Too-Tall. "Look out below!"

The class broke up laughing. Milton sighed and sank back into his chair as Teacher Bob motioned for quiet.

"Good talk, Milt," said Too-Tall. *"Heavy."*

Things didn't go any better for Milton in gym class later that day. The cubs were right in the middle of a two-week gymnastics program, and today was the day for vaulting the horse. Milton took one look at the imposing apparatus and gulped. But Mr.

Grizzmeyer, the gym teacher, insisted that everyone give it a try. Brother vaulted first while Mr. Grizzmeyer spotted for him, and he cleared the horse with room to spare. Then Brother replaced the teacher as spotter for the rest of the cubs. Everyone cleared the horse without a hitch, except for Babs Bruno, who caught a foot on the apparatus and tumbled off to one side. Luckily, Brother was a good spotter and caught her before she hurt herself.

Meanwhile, Milton kept moving backward rather than forward in line, letting

other cubs go ahead of him. Finally, there was no one left in line but Milton. He took a deep breath and readied himself for an awkward run at the horse.

But now that Mr. Grizzmeyer had taken a closer look at the new cub, he was having his doubts about Brother's ability to spot for him. Clearly someone bigger and stronger was needed. Just then, out of the corner of his eye, he noticed Too-Tall and the gang sneaking off across the gym. (They had a habit of trying to leave early.) "Hey, you guys!" he barked. "Where do you think you're going?"

Too-Tall grinned and said, "I think we'll observe this one from a safer distance, if you don't mind, Mr. G."

"Well, I *do* mind!" snapped Mr. Grizzmeyer. "Get back over here. In fact, Too-Tall, I want you to replace Brother as spotter."

"Replace *who* as *what?*" asked Too-Tall in mock horror. "Are you tryin' to get me killed?"

The cubs all laughed. All except Milton and Bertha.

"Quit bellyaching and do it," ordered Mr. Grizzmeyer.

Winking at the class, Too-Tall strutted over to the horse and took up his position. With supreme confidence, he called, "Okay, Miltie! Let 'er rip!"

Milton took another massive breath and lumbered toward the horse. When he was

about halfway there, some of the cubs
noticed that the look of confidence on Too-
Tall's face had vanished. And as Milton
planted his hands on the horse's handles
and, with legs spread wide, thrust his enormous body into the air, Too-Tall looked as if
he might panic. But he didn't. When both
of Milton's huge feet hit the horse, causing

him to pitch forward, Too-Tall rushed to catch him.

Milton hit the mat with a resounding thud. Actually, it was more complicated than that: Milton hit Too-Tall, and *Too-Tall,* with Milton on top of him, hit the mat with a resounding thud.

"Wow!" said Barry Bruin as the new cub picked himself up amid much laughter from the class. "Maybe we could get Milton a job in a pancake restaurant!"

This time it wasn't only Milton and Bertha who didn't laugh. Too-Tall was quiet, too. As the bell rang ending the period, he peeled himself off the mat and stomped off toward the exit, without even inviting his gang to follow.

As the rest of the class headed for the exit, too, Mr. Grizzmeyer hurried over to Milton. "I like the way you carry that weight, son," he said brightly. "We could sure use a hefty lad like you on our football and basketball teams."

"Yeah!" said Skuzz. "We need a *wide* body in the low post in basketball."

"And he could play *wide* receiver on the football team!" cracked Smirk.

"No way!" said Vinnie. "He should play offensive end. 'Cause he has the most *offensive end* of any cub in the school!"

"That's enough out of you three!" snapped Mr. Grizzmeyer. "Don't listen to those bums," he told Milton.

But the damage had been done. Milton was already trudging toward the exit. It looked as if he didn't want to have anything to do with school sports.

Chapter 3
Family Discussion

The fact that Too-Tall rather than Milton had gotten the worst of Milton's horse vault was bad news for Milton. At afternoon recess, Too-Tall was on the new cub's case even worse than before. Brother and his friends watched in disgust as the gang hurled a steady stream of abuse at their victim.

That evening, at the Bear family's dinner table, Papa brought up the subject of Farmer Ben's new hired hands. He wondered if they had any children.

"Sure do," said Sister. "Milton Chubb. Which is a real kick, because he's the chubbiest cub in the school. Isn't that hilarious?"

"It's not funny, Sis," said Brother.

"Hey, what happened to your sense of humor?" chided Sister.

"I'll admit it must seem funny if you've never seen the poor guy in action," said Brother. "But if you'd seen what I saw today in Teacher Bob's class, in gym class, and on the playground, you might be crying instead of laughing."

"Oh, dear," said Mama. "That bad?"

Brother nodded. He told them all about the girls teasing Milton and Too-Tall getting on his case with a vengeance.

"Sounds pretty rough," said Papa. "There aren't many cubs who'll stand up to Too-Tall."

"That's just what I've been thinking," said Brother. "I'm just about the only cub who's ever succeeded at it. That's why I'm gonna confront Too-Tall tomorrow morning. I'll tell him that if he doesn't lay off Milton, he'll have to fight me."

"Are you kidding?" said Sister. "I hear Too-Tall's still furious at Milton for falling on him in gym class. I don't think he'll back down. And that means *you'll* get beat up!"

"Then so be it," said Brother grimly. "*Somebody* has to put a stop to this nonsense."

Mama, Papa, and Sister looked at Brother in astonishment. They had never seen him so determined about anything before.

Finally Papa said, "It's very noble of you to take one on the chin for a cub you hardly know, Brother. But I wonder if you've given enough thought to finding a way to solve this problem short of violence."

"Papa's right, dear," said Mama. "Besides, solving Milton's problem for him might make it that much harder for him to earn the respect of other cubs. Wouldn't it be better for Milton if you could find a way to help him solve his own problem?"

Brother thought for a moment. He nodded. "I see what you mean, Mama. But I

don't see how he could solve it. He's such a
wimp."

"Now, wait just a minute," said Mama.
"Nothing you've told us about Milton sug-
gests he's *afraid* of Too-Tall. He might just
be shy and soft-spoken. That doesn't make
him a wimp."

"Hmm," said Brother. "You might be
right again. Come to think of it, he didn't
seem afraid of Too-Tall on the playground.
He did a lot of looking down out of embar-
rassment. But he didn't even flinch when
Too-Tall put his hand on his shoulder and
dubbed him Massive Milton."

"There you are!" said Papa. "You don't
know this cub well enough to say whether

or not he can solve the problem. It seems to me that the first step to helping him is getting to know him better. Why don't you pay Farmer Ben a visit after school tomorrow, son?"

Brother looked puzzled for a moment. Then he caught on. "Oh!" he said. "You mean as an excuse to pay *Milton* a visit!"

"Exactly," said Papa. "At Farmer Ben's he'll be on his own turf. He's bound to be more comfortable there than at school. He might open up a little."

"And being with him on the farm," said Mama, "will give you an opportunity to mention Bertha Broom—how she grew up on a farm, too. I think there's a chance for a real friendship between those two."

"Why think small?" said Sister. "They might even wind up going steady!"

"Not so fast, Sis," said Brother. "What

Milton needs most right now is a friend. Oh, wait. I just realized. Bertha isn't in the picture anyway. She's too busy right now to make any new friends. She's not only fullback on the football team, she's also heavyweight on Coach Grizzmeyer's new wrestling team. Wrestling season won't start until winter, but they're already practicing and training every day after football practice and on weekends, too."

"I've been meaning to ask you about that," said Papa. "When will Mr. G hear from the league about whether or not the new team has been accepted?"

"Should be any day now," said Brother. "And if the answer's yes, Bertha just won't have time for Milton."

"Oh, *please*," scoffed Sister. "Sister Bear's first rule of romance: If a girl really likes a boy, she'll *make* time for him."

Brother's eyebrows rose. It seemed his little sister was growing up.

Chapter 4
A Budding Friendship

Though Sister had always enjoyed playing matchmaker, she agreed with Brother that what Milton needed most was a good friend, not a girlfriend. Besides, she thought, with two shy cubs like Milton and Bertha, the best a matchmaker could do was get them to talk to each other—and then let nature take its course. So she suggested that Brother ask Bonnie to call Bertha that evening and talk to her about Milton. Bonnie could ask her to introduce herself to Milton on the school playground the next morning.

"But Bertha's so shy," said Brother. "Are you sure she'll do it?"

"She may be shy," said Sister, "but she's also one of the most kindhearted cubs I know. When Bonnie explains how badly Milton needs a friend, she'll do it."

Sister's suggestion worked. On the playground the next morning, Brother managed to interrupt Queenie, Bermuda, and Babs in their teasing of Milton by telling Queenie that they'd heard a rumor that Too-Tall had a secret crush on someone. As soon as Milton was alone, Bertha went up to him and introduced herself.

The two were still talking pleasantly, if a bit shyly, when Too-Tall and his gang finally arrived on the playground. Ordinarily, this would have broken up Milton and Bertha's conversation. But today Too-Tall didn't have a chance to make fun of Milton. Queenie,

his on-again, off-again girlfriend, immediately cornered him and lit into him about his secret crush. Too-Tall was taken completely by surprise, because he hadn't heard the rumor yet. He couldn't have. Brother and Bonnie had made it up just minutes earlier on their way to school.

Now, getting Queenie mad at Too-Tall by starting a rumor is a good way to distract Too-Tall from teasing someone. But it's just as good a way to get *Too-Tall* mad at *you*. Fortunately, Brother had taken care of this possibility. After checking with Harry McGill, he had told Queenie that he'd heard the rumor from Harry, who had gotten an E-mail message about it on his computer the night before. Whoever had sent the message hadn't left a name, probably out of fear of Too-Tall's wrath. Brother hoped that this phony story would keep

Too-Tall from ever finding out who started the rumor.

Sure enough, Too-Tall spent all three recesses that day questioning cubs about the rumor. By the end of the day, not only had he failed to find out who had started it, he had also spent so much time questioning cubs that he never had a chance to tease Milton. And that gave Milton and Bertha more time to get to know each other.

Chapter 5
On His Own Turf

After football practice that day, Brother headed for Farmer Ben's. He was very pleased with how things had gone at school between Milton and Bertha. It seemed they were already well on their way to becoming friends. At the same time, he knew that rough times lay ahead for them. Soon Too-Tall would give up trying to solve the rumor case and return to business as usual. That meant that Milton needed more than one friend.

At the farmhouse, Farmer Ben greeted Brother and told him that Milton had just headed out to the barn to pitch hay. Brother walked over to the barn and went in. Milton, pitchfork in hand, stood before a huge pile of hay.

"Hi, Milton," said Brother.

Milton looked up and frowned. "I know you," he drawled. "You're that Brother Bear fella I met yesterday mornin'. I never expected to see *you* here."

At first Brother didn't know what Milton meant. Then, all of a sudden, he understood. "Oh!" he said. "You mean because of what I said when we were introduced?"

Milton gave a slight nod of the head and kept his eyes on Brother.

"Look, Milton," said Brother. "That's one of the reasons I came. I want to apologize. It was an accident. It just sort of...slipped out."

Milton kept staring at Brother for a while. Then his frown eased. "I may not be as clever as you city cubs," he said. "But I can tell when a fella's bein' truthful. I accept your apology."

"Thanks," said Brother. "What're ya doin'?"

"I was just gettin' set to pitch this here hay up into the hayloft," said Milton.

"Mind if I watch?"

"Nope," said Milton. And with that, he got a good grip on his pitchfork and began flinging great heaps of hay into the hayloft with incredible speed. Within minutes he

had reduced the enormous pile of hay on the barn floor to a few scattered strands.

Brother gazed up at the full hayloft. "Wow!" he said. "I've never seen such powerful arms and shoulders on a cub!"

Milton cracked a smile. "Aw, shucks," he said. "Always been strong. Ever since I was knee high to a grasshopper, I guess."

Brother knew it was only an expression, but it was hard to imagine Milton ever having been a little cub at all. "I tried pitching hay once," he said, "but I couldn't even reach the loft. You know, some of my friends and I worked part time as farmhands for Farmer Ben for a while."

"Yeah, I know," said Milton. "That Bertha gal told me."

"Oh, Bertha Broom," said Brother. "She's real nice, isn't she?"

Milton gave Brother a suspicious look. "Come on outside with me," he said. "Gotta replace a broken fence post." As they walked, he continued, "Yeah, Bertha's kinda nice, I guess. Got to talkin' to her today at recess. Don't s'pose I woulda if that little bully fella hadn't quit pesterin' me."

"Little bully fella?" said Brother. "Oh, you mean Too-Tall."

"Yeah, that one."

"Well, I think I should warn you," said Brother. "Too-Tall was sort of distracted today by a problem with his girlfriend, Queenie. Tomorrow he might be back on your case. And if you're with Bertha, he'll be that much harder on you."

Milton shrugged and hefted a heavy wooden fence post. "I can take whatever foolishness that little fella dishes out," he said. "Just so he leaves Bertha alone." He lifted the post above his head and plunged it into the ground. Then he picked up a sledgehammer and gave the post a couple of mighty whacks.

Brother might have just stood there gaping at this remarkable show of strength had he not been absorbed in thinking about what Milton had just said. "Fat chance," he replied before he could catch himself, then stammered, "Er, uh...I mean there's not much chance of that. Too-Tall's bound to be just as hard on Bertha as he is on you."

Milton's grip tightened around the handle of the sledgehammer. "He better not make fun of Bertha," he said. "I won't stand for that."

Brother was surprised to see that the gentle giant had a temper, after all. "What'll you do if Too-Tall makes fun of Bertha?" he asked.

"What'll I do?" said Milton. "Why, I'll—" But he didn't finish the sentence. Instead, he raised the sledgehammer again and

pounded the fence post deeper into the ground with a series of savage blows. Then he straightened up, wiped his brow with a forearm, and said, "Better not say. Why worry about somethin' that hasn't even happened yet?"

"Why, indeed?" said Brother. "Well, Milton, nice talkin' to you. Gotta go."

"See ya around, little fella," said Milton. He turned and walked off toward the barn.

Hmm, thought Brother as he headed back across the cow pasture. Could it be that Massive Milton was already getting a crush on Bertha Broom? And was it possible that when Too-Tall insulted Bertha, Milton would treat him the same way he'd treated that fence post?

Chapter 6
A Shocking Decision

Meanwhile, at Bear Country School, something was about to happen that would have a big impact on Milton Chubb's life. Coach Grizzmeyer's new wrestling team had just started practicing in the gym. Practices were always held after football practice so that Bertha and Too-Tall could attend. They were fullback and tight end on the football team, and on the wrestling team they were heavyweight and light heavyweight. Barry Bruin at middleweight and Gil Grizzwold at lightweight rounded out the wrestling team.

Coach Grizzmeyer didn't mind making special scheduling arrangements so the school could start a wrestling team. He was a great fan of the sport. He had been a star wrestler himself right through college, and his greatest ambition now was to place a

team in the well-established school league. In fact, he had even handed over the football team's head coaching job to his assistant, Teacher Bob, that year so he could put in extra time coaching wrestling.

"Good takedown, Bertha!" barked Mr. Grizzmeyer. "Better help Barry up. He looks a little woozy."

Despite Bertha's helping hand, Barry stumbled and fell flat on his face. He looked up wearily. "It's no use, Coach," he said. "I just can't give Bertha a decent practice match. She really needs Too-Tall to go against."

Mr. Grizzmeyer glanced at his wristwatch. "Where *is* that slacker? Football practice was over at least twenty minutes ago!"

"I don't think he's coming, Coach," said Bertha. "He cut football practice, too. Said something about investigating a nasty rumor."

Just then Teacher Bob poked his head out of the gym office and called, "Coach! Phone for you! It's the president of the wrestling league!"

Mr. Grizzmeyer's eyes lit up. "He must be calling to welcome our team to the league!" he said, and hurried to the office, with his three wrestlers close on his heels. He snatched up the phone and said, "Hello, Mr. Grapple. Grizzmeyer here. I just want to say it's a great honor to accept your gracious offer to join the league. I can assure you that the Bear Country School wrestling team will be a worthy addition to—." He broke off. A look of horror came over him. "What? *Unacceptable?* You can't mean that! Why?" As he listened, the horror turned to shock. "*No girls allowed?* No, I *didn't*

know...I just assumed you'd done away with that silly rule like all the other school leagues...Yes, I *know* I tried to keep Bertha off the football team. But that was then, and this is now! I've changed! And so should you, I might add, and those other guys who made up the league rules—hello? Hello? *Hello?*"

Coach Grizzmeyer slammed the phone down and looked at the cubs in amazement. "He hung up on me! Can you believe that?"

But now all the air seemed to go out of him. His shoulders slumped. "Well, you all heard what happened. They won't accept us unless we replace Bertha with a boy."

Bertha hung her head. Barry stared at the wall. Gil asked, "What do we do now, Coach?"

I'LL TELL YOU WHAT WE DO. WE FIGHT!

Mr. Grizzmeyer stood straight up and squared his shoulders again. "I'll tell you what we do," he said. "We fight! We can't allow them to keep girls off our wrestling team, not in this day and age! Besides, Bertha's our best wrestler! We'll take 'em to court!"

But Bertha shook her head. She was the kind of cub who hates being the center of attention. "Please, Coach," she said. "Don't make a big fuss on my account. I'd really rather not be in a league that feels that way about girl wrestlers."

Though the fire remained in Mr. Grizzmeyer's eyes, he pursed his lips and nodded. "All right, Bertha," he said. "If that's the way you want it, then that's the way it's gonna be. But I can't think of a replacement for you. I guess we just won't have a wrestling team this year."

Suddenly Bertha had an idea. "I know!" she said. "What about that new cub, Milton Chubb? Couldn't he replace me?"

"Yeah!" said Barry. "There sure isn't any question about his being a heavyweight."

The coach considered this for only a moment before shaking his head no. He thought the new cub was too gentle, too passive to play any competitive sport. Besides, he'd heard that Too-Tall was giving him a pretty rough time. Judging from Milton's reaction to the gang's taunts about his joining the football team or the basketball team, it wasn't likely he'd want to be on the same team with Too-Tall.

As the dejected cubs trudged off to the locker room, Barry turned to Gil and said, "Pretty disgusting deal, huh?"

"Yeah," said Gil. "But Coach still has that fire in his eyes. He's a fighter. And he wants

this wrestling team more than anything."

"But he promised Bertha he wouldn't do anything," said Barry.

"Not exactly," Gil pointed out. "He promised *not to make a big fuss.*"

"So what?" said Barry. "Can you imagine Coach fighting for something *without* making a big fuss?"

As it turned out, however, Barry had underestimated his coach. For at that very moment, Mr. Grizzmeyer was on the phone in the gym office. "Now, Queenie," he was saying, "I think we can win this case in court, maybe even in time to meet this year's league deadline for new teams. But I promised Bertha there wouldn't be any fuss. That means *you* have to promise *me* that you won't start a public campaign like you did to get Bertha onto the football team. Okay? Good. Let's get down to business. I happen to know that your cousin Bermuda's big sister is a lawyer. And I also know she used to work in Judge Gavel's office as his assistant…"

Chapter 7
The Sleeping Giant Wakes!

And so a court challenge to the wrestling league's no-girls rule was set in motion. Coach Grizzmeyer hoped that the friendly relationship between Judge Gavel and Bermuda's sister would lead to an early hearing date in court. But the start of the wrestling season was less than three weeks away. As the coach looked out at cubs gathering on the school playground the next morning from his office window, he was beginning to doubt that the court case could be speeded up enough to meet the league deadline for new teams.

Out on the playground, Brother and Bonnie were pondering their own problem. So far, there was no sign that Too-Tall had figured out the trick they'd played on him. But there was no guarantee that that wouldn't change as soon as the big guy reached school.

"There he is now," said Brother. "He just came through the gate."

"Uh-oh," said Bonnie. "He's coming over here. Try to look casual."

"Well, well," said Too-Tall, approaching at the head of his gang. "Look what the cat dragged in. Or should I say, 'Look what the *kitten* dragged in'?"

"Hi, big guy," said Brother. "What's up?"

"I'll tell you what's up," sneered Too-Tall. "Had a little talk with Cool Carl King last night. You know that so-called rumor you said Wheels McGill got off his computer?

Cool was gonna play computer chess with Wheels that night. But he couldn't. Know why? 'Cause there was a power failure in the whole neighborhood. Which is the same neighborhood that Wheels lives in, by the way. And it lasted *until the next morning.*"

Brother and Bonnie glanced at each

other. "Gee," said Brother. "Must have been the night before…"

"Nice try," said Too-Tall. "It wasn't the night before. Or any other night. And don't try to blame it on Wheels. 'Cause I figured out that it was *you two* who masterminded this prank. And I even figured out *why* you did it." He pointed across the schoolyard to where Milton and Bertha stood apart from the other cubs, talking happily as if in a world of their own. "You did it to get me off

YOU'RE GONNA HAVE TO BEAT ME UP, TOO!

Massive Milton's case for a while, so those two lovebirds—or should I say love*whales*—could spend some quality time together."

"Okay, you figured it out," said Brother. He put up his fists. "I'm not afraid of you. Go ahead. Beat me up."

Sister, who had overheard, sprang forward, fists at the ready. "You're gonna have to beat me up, too!" she cried. "I didn't know about the prank, but *I'm* the real matchmaker behind all this!"

Too-Tall laughed. "Figures. Sister *Cupid* Bear strikes again. Put your dukes down, both of ya. I ain't gonna beat nobody up."

"You're not?" Brother and Sister said in unison.

"Nah," said Too-Tall. "That would be *uncivilized*."

Brother, Sister, and Bonnie gave each other puzzled looks.

"I got a better way of getting back at you bums," continued Too-Tall. With an evil grin, he looked across the schoolyard again. "Since the reason you did it was to get Milton and Bertha together, I'm gonna go over there and *break 'em up!* I'm gonna embarrass 'em so bad, they won't even *look* at each other for the rest of their long, overweight lives! Let's go to work, gang!"

Queenie, who had also overheard, made a move to run after the gang to stop them. But Brother caught her by the arm. "Chill out," he said.

"But they're gonna break up a beautiful romance!" said Queenie. "Someone's gotta stop them!" As always, Queenie had a soft spot in her heart for cubs with crushes.

"Not necessary," said Brother calmly. "Something tells me Milton can handle this all by himself."

By now Too-Tall and the gang were dancing around Milton and Bertha in a circle, taunting, "Massive Milton's no darn good, the fattest guy in the neighborhood!" Milton just folded his arms and watched. After

a while they switched to a new taunt: "Milt works on the farm every day, makes ten cents an hour and that ain't *hay!*" Still Milton ignored them.

"You call that *handling* it?" wailed Queenie. "If he keeps handling it like that, he'll be the size of a mouse by the time they're through!"

"Keep your blouse on," said Brother. "Wait till they say something about Bertha."

At that very moment the gang stopped dancing, gathered in a row right in front of their victims, and began a new chant.

"Milt is massive,

Bertha's big.

We call them

Mr. and Mrs. Pig!"

Milton's mild face suddenly scrunched into a furious frown. He unfolded his enormous arms and reached for the gang. Grab-

bing them by their collars, two by two—
Too-Tall and Skuzz in one massive hand,
Smirk and Vinnie in the other—he lifted
them, wriggling and squirming, high into

the air and let them fall to the hardtop in a pile of tangled arms and legs. To finish the job, he lunged forward and did a belly flop on the pile.

A hush had fallen over the playground. Every cub present stared at Milton in awe as he calmly picked himself up off the pile of pancaked bullies and walked back to Bertha's side.

At his office window, Mr. Grizzmeyer was also staring at Milton. What a cub! He

seemed so gentle and shy, but when he got riled up, he had the strength of an ox and the temper of a Brahma bull!

Suddenly a vision came to the coach. It was a vision of something that would not only solve his problem with the school wrestling league but probably win a championship for the team. A vision of Massive Milton Chubb, in a Bear Country School wrestling uniform, performing his special move, the "pancake," on every heavyweight in the league!

Chapter 8
A New Life

From that day on, Massive Milton's life changed for the better. When Mr. Grizzmeyer told him how he could save the school wrestling team, he joined in an instant. That gave as big a boost to his popularity with the other cubs as his victory over Too-Tall had.

Milton liked the idea of becoming a star heavyweight wrestler. And now, of course, there was no question of his being afraid to be on the same team with Too-Tall. In fact, Too-Tall starting cutting wrestling practice to avoid Milton. Whenever he passed Milton on the playground, he would cringe, give a sheepish grin, and tip his cap.

Milton had a lot of work to do if he was going to become a star wrestler in time for the first league match. Coach Grizzmeyer put him on a crash training course. Every day, before wrestling practice, the coach personally supervised Milton's training. Milton did sit-ups, push-ups, and pull-ups till he was blue in the face. He tried jumping jacks in the gym, but as soon as Mr. G noticed the rafters shaking, he took Milton out to the football field, joking that "crash course" was, after all, just an expression.

There he had Milton finish his jumping jacks and do some wind sprints. (Actually, the wind sprinted and Milton just ran.) After a full week of conditioning, Massive Milton wasn't quite as massive anymore, having taken off a few pounds.

Of course, there's more to wrestling than conditioning, brute strength, and the "pancake." During practice, Coach Grizzmeyer showed Milton all the classic moves. They worked on his quickness and timing, too. The coach asked Bertha to give Milton some practice matches, but she just blushed and said she didn't feel right about it. So Mr. G squeezed into his old college wrestling uniform and gave Milton some practice matches himself.

Mr. Grizzmeyer didn't know what Bertha had meant by "not feeling right" about wrestling Milton. But by now all the cubs knew that Milton had asked Bertha to go to the big school dance with him the following week. Some started joking that while Milton was on a crash course, Milton and Bertha were on a *crush* course.

Chapter 9
Two Rights Make a Wrong

After a while, Too-Tall came slinking back to wrestling practice. Coach Grizzmeyer had gotten ahold of him and given him an earful. Even so, Too-Tall managed to get the coach to agree not to put him up against Massive Milton in practice. The coach didn't mind making such a deal, because his own wrestling uniform already fit him a lot better now. Wrestling Milton day after day at practice had caused him to take off a few pounds himself.

Finally, there were only a few days left before the first league wrestling match of the year. At the last practice before the match, the team looked to be in excellent shape. Especially Milton. His continued conditioning had taken off more pounds. Compared to how he looked before, he was slim and trim.

As Coach Grizzmeyer wrestled Milton, he could tell that the weight loss had caused the big cub to lose some of his brute strength. But what he had lost in power was more than made up for by what he had gained in quickness and endurance. Now the once massive cub was a lean, mean wrestling machine.

Just as Coach Grizzmeyer was motioning that he needed a breather, the far door of the gym swung open, and in walked Queenie, Brother, Sister, Cousin Fred, Bonnie, and Bertha. Actually, only Queenie, Brother, Sister, Fred, and Bonnie were walking. Bertha was being dragged and pushed by the others.

"What's going on?" yelled Mr. Grizzmeyer. "Stop bearhandling that cub this instant!"

"Chill out, Coach," said Queenie. "When we got to the gym door, she suddenly turned shy about claiming what's rightly hers."

"What's rightly hers?" said Grizzmeyer. "What on earth are you talking about?"

Queenie raised a fist in the air. "We won!" she cried. "Bermuda's sister won the court case! Judge Gavel just struck down the wrestling league's no-girls rule!"

The coach's mouth fell open in surprise. He had gotten so caught up in getting Massive Milton ready for the wrestling season that he had completely forgotten about the court case! What was more, it looked as if Queenie and the few friends she had told about it had done such a good job keeping it a secret that Bertha had only just found out about it.

Mr. Grizzmeyer now pondered his two most important recent accomplishments as wrestling coach. First, he had gotten Massive Milton into top wrestling form for the start of the season. Second, he had set in motion a successful legal challenge to the league's old-fashioned rules. Taken separately, these were great things for his team. But taken together...

Mr. G knew well the old saying "Two wrongs don't make a right." But he had never heard anyone say that two rights couldn't make a wrong. Now he knew why.

"Er...uh...," stammered the coach, "...it seems we are confronted with a dilemma..."

"A what?" said Sister.

"Dilemma," said Cousin Fred, who read

the dictionary for fun. "A situation requiring a choice between equally undesirable alternatives."

"Hey!" said Queenie. "Don't call Bertha 'undesirable'!"

"You don't understand, Queenie," said

Coach Grizzmeyer. "What's undesirable is leaving either of these two fine wrestlers off the team."

But Queenie wasn't satisfied. "There's no dilemma!" she insisted. "Bertha was the team heavyweight first!"

"Wait just a minute!" said Too-Tall, seeing a chance to get on Milton's good side. "Milton has worked real hard to get ready for the season. *He's* our heavyweight now!"

Queenie and Too-Tall began shouting at each other at the top of their lungs. Soon they were joined by the other cubs. The yelling went on until Coach Grizzmeyer put his whistle between his lips and blew one piercing blast. *"Qui-e-e-t-t!"* he roared. Instant silence. "The way I see it, both Bertha and Milton have an equal claim on the heavyweight spot on this wrestling team."

But Bertha said, "That's okay, Coach. I don't deserve it as much as Milton does." She was blushing.

Milton quickly put in, "Oh, no, Coach. *I* don't deserve it. *Bertha* does." He was blushing, too.

Queenie noticed their red faces and cooed, "Oh, isn't that *sweet…*"

Mr. Grizzmeyer blew another blast on his whistle. "That's enough mush at my wrestling practice!" he barked. "Sweet or not, it makes no difference. Like I said, Bertha and Milton *both* deserve the heavyweight spot."

"Then how do we decide who gets it?" asked Barry.

"There's only one fair way," said the coach. "They'll have to wrestle for it."

Now the blushing got really intense. So intense, in fact, that Sister could almost see a red glow spread through the gym. "Wow," she said softly to Brother. "When I decided to play matchmaker, I had no idea it would lead to *this* kind of match."

"No kidding!" blurted out big-mouth Queenie, who had overheard. "It's a *love match!*"

Chapter 10
Let's Get It On!

Queenie's remark made Bertha and Milton blush so hard that the others could almost feel the temperature rise in the gym. But the two cubs had no choice. Coach Grizzmeyer declared that he could not have a wrestling team if the heavyweight spot were not decided fairly.

So Bertha went to the locker room to put on her uniform. When she returned, she took her place at one corner of the wrestling mat. Milton stood at the other corner, and Coach Grizzmeyer was in the middle.

The other cubs had climbed into the stands to watch and root. "Go, Broom!" cried Queenie. "Sweep him under the mat!" Too-Tall countered with "When does a Broom turn into a pancake? When Massive Milton pins her!"

But Brother, Sister, Bonnie, and Cousin Fred didn't know which cub to root for. They hated to see either lose. And Sister the matchmaker was beginning to worry that the Love Match might lead to a breakup. "I wonder," she said to Brother. "If Milton pins Bertha now, will she let him pin her at the big dance tonight?"

Queenie overheard again. "Did he buy her a pin already?" she gasped.

"That's the rumor," said Sister.

Queenie was suddenly torn between rooting for Bertha and not rooting at all. But only for a moment. "There are larger issues involved here than whether or not two cubs go steady!" she declared. "Since there has to be a winner, let it be a female! Go, Bertha!"

"Are you kiddin'?" said Too-Tall. "A girl can't beat a guy at *wrestling!* Milton's gonna pancake her so flat, they'll have to pour maple syrup on her to revive her!"

"All right, wrestling fans!" boomed Coach Grizzmeyer. "We have fifteen minutes of heavyweight wrestling for your enjoyment! In one corner, wearing the Bear Country School team uniform: Big Bertha Broom! In the other corner, wearing the...uh...the

other Bear Country School team uniform: Massive Milton Chubb! *Let's get it on!*" And with that, he blew his whistle to start the match.

What followed was a grueling exhibition of wrestling power and skill. If anyone had

thought that the two heavyweight con-
tenders wouldn't try their hardest because
of their mutual crush, they were soon
proved wrong. Both cubs did themselves
proud. By the time Coach Grizzmeyer's
whistle signaled the end of the match, the
grapplers each had two takedowns and two
escapes.

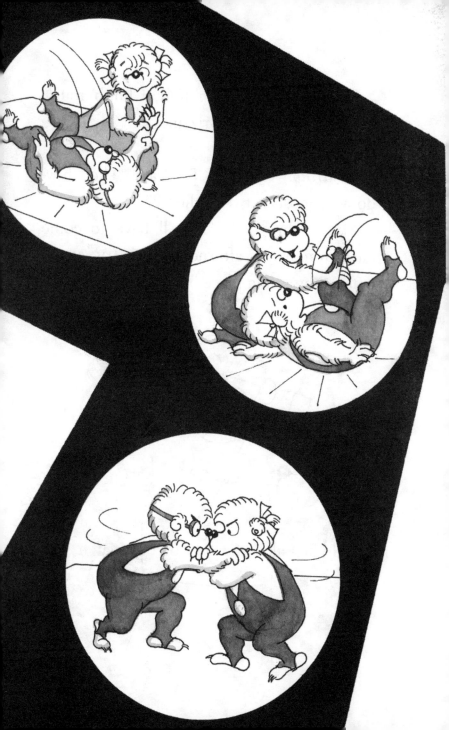

"Final score: Broom four, Chubb four!" announced Coach Grizzmeyer. "I declare this match a draw!"

"A *draw?*" moaned Too-Tall. "Then how do we choose between them?"

Mr. G shrugged. "They'll have to come back tomorrow afternoon and try again. Same time, same place."

Chapter 11
Pancake, Anyone?

What a letdown! Everyone would have to wait a whole day to find out who would be the team's heavyweight.

Milton and Bertha still sat on the mat, breathing hard. They were exhausted. Maybe that's why they weren't blushing. Or maybe...

"Gee," Sister whispered to Brother, "do you think this match crushed their crush?"

"Either this match or the one hanging over their heads," said Brother. "Somehow, I don't think we'll be seeing them together at the dance tonight."

"All right, cubs," said Coach Grizzmeyer, heading toward the office. "See you all back here tomorrow."

"Wait a minute, Coach," said Bertha. She was looking strangely at Milton.

"What is it?" asked Mr. G.

"Milton's lost an awful lot of weight," she said.

"Thanks to my training program," said the coach proudly. "He may be the best-conditioned heavyweight in the division now."

"But I'm not even sure he *is* a heavy-weight anymore," said Bertha.

Coach Grizzmeyer looked carefully at Milton. Then he had Milton and Bertha stand side by side. "Hmm," he said. "I hadn't thought of that. Only one way to find out for sure."

In one corner of the gym stood a scale

the school athletes used for weighing themselves. The cubs crowded around it as Milton stepped onto it and Mr. G adjusted the measuring weights. The coach leaned forward to peer at the measuring bar. "Well, I'll be!" he said. "He's a fraction of a pound too light!"

"Yay!" cried Queenie. "That makes Bertha our team's heavyweight!"

"And if I know my wrestling divisions," said Cousin Fred, "it makes Milton a *light* heavyweight."

All eyes turned to Too-Tall. Barry said what everyone was thinking: "But we already *have* a light heavyweight!"

Coach Grizzmeyer looked from Milton to Too-Tall and back. "There's only one fair way to decide who gets the light heavy-weight spot on the team," he said. "You two cubs will have to—"

But Too-Tall cut him off. "Hold on, Coach," he said, backing slowly toward an exit. There was fear in the big guy's eyes.

"What's wrong now?" asked the coach.

"I...er, uh...I've been meaning to tell you, Coach," stammered Too-Tall, still inching his way toward the exit. "I think I oughta concentrate on football and basketball this year...wrestling kinda ruins my concentration..." Suddenly he stopped and looked at the unbelieving stares of his audience. "Oh, what's the use. The truth is, *I'm allergic to pancakes.*" And with that, he turned and strode to the exit.

Milton and Bertha beamed at each other as Coach Grizzmeyer said, "Well, that settles it. Bear Country School has a wrestling team."

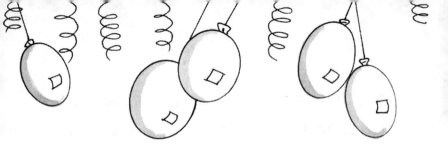

Chapter 12
You Light Up My Life

At the big dance that evening, rockin' cubs packed the gym floor the instant the music started. But not Brother, Sister, Bonnie, and Queenie. They were all too busy watching the main entrance.

Soon Too-Tall strutted over and grabbed Queenie's arm. "Come on, girl!" he shouted above the din. "Let's rock!"

"Can't!" Queenie yelled back. "Gotta watch for Bertha and Milton! They haven't arrived yet!"

"You and your romance!" moaned Too-Tall. "Why don't you just leave those two alone?"

"Leave them alone?" said Queenie. "Who are *you* to talk about leaving them alone?"

Too-Tall had no ready comeback for Queenie's gibe. Grumbling, he slunk off.

"I don't think they're coming," said Sister sadly. "What a shame."

But just then Queenie pointed at the entrance. "Here they are!" she cried. "And look what's on Bertha's blouse! I guess he couldn't wait to get to the dance to pin her."

Sure enough, what Milton had failed to

do that afternoon on the wrestling mat he
had done in his parents' car on the way to
the dance. Sister "Cupid" Bear beamed
with pride.

"That's great!" said Bonnie. "Now we can
dance!"

The cubs danced till they nearly dropped—Brother with Bonnie, Queenie with Too-Tall, and Sister with her best friend, Lizzy Bruin. Then they headed for the refreshments table as slow music came on for a change of pace.

"Let's sit this one out," Brother said to Bonnie. "Rest up for when the rock music comes back on."

"Good idea," said Sister. "Hey, where's Queenie?"

"Probably still dancing with Too-Tall," said Bonnie.

HEY, WHAT'S THAT STRANGE RED LIGHT?

In fact, Queenie was not dancing with Too-Tall anymore. At that moment, she was on the other side of the gym, coaxing Bertha and Milton onto the dance floor.

"Hey, what's that strange red light?" asked Sister after a while.

The cubs looked around. A faint red glow had spread through the darkened gym.

Brother gazed up into the rafters. "I don't see any red lamps...," he said.

"It seems to be coming from the dance floor," said Bonnie.

The cubs turned their attention to the dance floor packed with cubs. Soon they saw what it was.

"Wow," said Sister. "I've heard of folks who light up a room when they come into it. But I always thought it was just an expression!"

There, in the middle of the crowd of

dancers, were Milton Chubb and Bertha Broom. They were dancing cheek to cheek. And blushing their hearts out.

It looked as though that afternoon's final whistle hadn't ended the Love Match, after all.

Stan and Jan Berenstain began writing and illustrating books for children in the early 1960s, when their two young sons were beginning to read. That marked the start of the best-selling Berenstain Bears series. Now, with more than one hundred books in print, videos, television shows, and even Berenstain Bears attractions at major amusement parks, it's hard to tell where the Bears end and the Berenstains begin!

Stan and Jan make their home in Bucks County, Pennsylvania, near their sons—Leo, a writer, and Michael, an illustrator—who are helping them with Big Chapter Books stories and pictures. They plan on writing and illustrating many more books for children, especially for their four grandchildren, who keep them well in touch with the kids of today.